For Delta V.
I love you to the Moon and back!
—Mommy

THIS BOOK BELONGS TO

It was the perfect night,
a million stars in the sky.

Perfect for a future astronaut like me.

"Time to come inside, Luna Muna!" called Mommy.

That's when I saw it! A shooting star streaking across the sky. I closed my eyes tight.

"I wish I could fly to space!"
I whispered.

I waited patiently.
Nothing happened.
I opened my eyes.
I was disappointed.

"I'm going to count to three,"
Mommy warned. She meant
business, so I blasted off inside.

"Goodnight, Luna Muna," said Mommy. "Dream big," said Daddy.

I closed my eyes and tried to sleep.

A bright light from my nightstand woke me up.
I peeked out from under my eye mask.
"Hey, who turned the lights on?" I asked.
But it wasn't my lamp. It was my space helmet!

I put it on. Something felt funny.

"Holy guacamole!" I yelled.

I was floating! Then I remembered everyone was still sleeping. "Holy Moly..." I whispered.

I floated carefully to the ceiling. Then down to the floor. Then up again. I was getting the hang of this astronaut business. I was a natural!

I did a push-up on one hand. Then one finger!

I pirouetted past my posters and cannonballed through the air.

I tried to twirl with Rover, but he wouldn't cooperate.

I decided to go exploring.

WHEEEEEEE!!

I did somersaults down the stairs.

I flew like Supergirl into the kitchen.

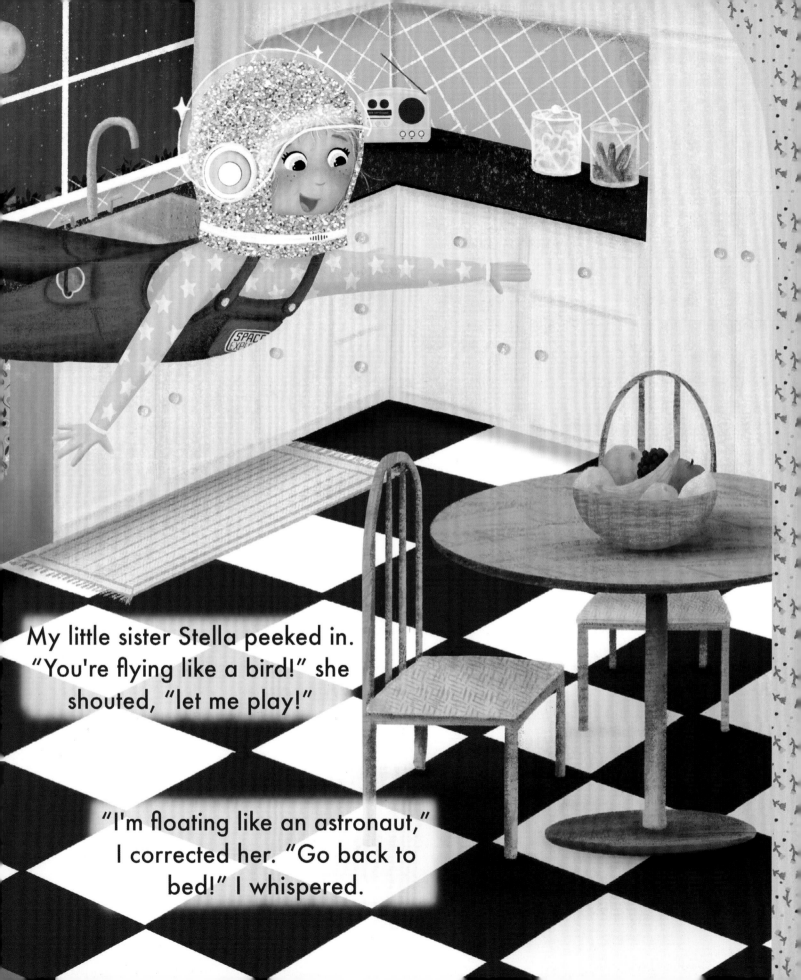

My little sister Stella peeked in. "You're flying like a bird!" she shouted, "let me play!"

"I'm floating like an astronaut," I corrected her. "Go back to bed!" I whispered.

I floated right up to the highest shelf and grabbed the cereal Mommy saves for special occasions. This was the most special occasion ever.

Then I quickly realized cereal might not be the best space snack. It floated in every direction.

"You made a gigantic mess!" said Stella, "I'm telling Mommy!"

Just then an idea hit me.
It was my best one ever.
"Follow me!" I told Stella.

I had a plan, but I was
going to need to jump high.
Really, really high.
I dashed to the backyard.

"Count me down, Stella!"
I called from the trampoline.

"Three...Two...One...

Blast Off!"

She yelled back.

I bounced harder than I'd
ever bounced before.

I floated up past the trees!
Up past the house!
Up past the clouds!
Up, up, up!

I zigged past an airplane!
I zagged past a spacecraft!
I zoomed past the
International Space Station!

Then I was there.

Luna Muna, the first little
girl on the Moon!

I bounced across craters. I twirled past a Moon Buggy.
I followed old footprints and made some new ones.

It was spacetastic—I could stay here
forever! And I had it all to myself.

Luna Muna, Queen of the Moon!

Then I saw the most beautiful thing I had ever seen.
Planet Earth was sparkling with bright blue oceans,
deep green forests, and ribbons of white clouds.

I tried to spot Mommy and Daddy and Stella, but
they were too small to see.

In fact, I couldn't see anybody. It was just me.
Queen Luna Muna, the only little girl on the Moon...

I started to feel a little bit lonely. I missed Mommy and
Daddy. I even missed Stella. It was time to go home.

I floated down. Down, down, down. Down past the Space Station, down past the spacecraft and the airplane.

Down past the clouds and the trees and the house. All the way down to my cozy bed.

"Turn off the lamp," Stella said.
"That's not the lamp!" I told her.
We both giggled.

Space is great, and I'm still going to be an astronaut one day, but there's no place like home.

Maybe next time I'll let Stella come, and we can explore space together.

MOON

It takes a nation to launch a moonshot!

More than 400,000 people worked on the Apollo Program, landing twelve men on the Moon from 1969–1972. In the coming years, NASA's Artemis Program will land the first woman and the next man!

There is no "dark side" of the Moon!

The "dark side" refers to the hemisphere of the Moon that's facing away from Earth, even though it gets just as much sunlight. Humans have only ever seen that "far side" from a spacecraft!

FACTS

Humans have left a lot of things on the Moon

In addition to rovers, flags, and footprints, lunar astronauts left behind tools, equipment, sentimental items, and yes, even bathroom waste! Leaving items behind made room for them to carry home precious Moon rocks!

The Moon is very old, but how it formed is a mystery!

One guess is that billions of years ago, something smashed into young Earth, and the debris from that big splat became our Moon!

You would weigh a lot less on the Moon than you do on Earth!

The Moon has much weaker gravitational pull than Earth, so you would weigh about one sixth of your weight on Earth...and could jump six times higher!

Published by DragonFruit, an imprint of
Mango Publishing, a division of Mango
Publishing Group, Inc.
Cover and Illustrations by: Allyson Wilson
Luna Muna. Library of Congress Cataloging-
in-Publication number: 2021941635
ISBN: (print) 978-1-64250-694-5 (ebook)
978-1-64250-695-2 BISAC category code:
JUV036010JUVENILE FICTION /
Technology / Astronauts & Space
Printed in China

AUTHOR

Kellie Gerardi is a researcher and science communicator who is flying to space on a dedicated science mission with Virgin Galactic. Her daughter, Delta, is very excited to watch Mommy become an astronaut!

ILLUSTRATOR

Allyson Wilson is a graphic designer and illustrator who loves creating fun environments full of detail (and thinks there's no such thing as too much sparkle)! She lives in Pennsylvania with her husband, Josh, and two shining stars, Felicity and Elliott.

LUNA MUNA
Space Café

3...2...1...Bake Sale! When Luna Muna's school hosts a bake sale fundraising competition, Luna opens her very own space café to serve out-of-this-world treats. Running a bakery isn't as easy as she expected, especially with such strong competition from her classmates. Just when everything is starting to look like one giant, galactic mess, Luna Muna discovers that teamwork and creative thinking just might be able to save the day...and the treats!

Look for Luna Muna: Space Café coming soon!

DragonFruit, an imprint of Mango Publishing, publishes high-quality children's books to inspire a love of lifelong learning in readers. DragonFruit publishes a variety of titles for kids, including children's picture books, nonfiction series, toddler activity books, pre-K activity books, science and education titles, and ABC books. Beautiful and engaging, our books celebrate diversity, spark curiosity, and capture the imaginations of parents and children alike. You can follow @DragonFruitKids on Instagram and @MangoPublishing on Twitter.